Why Heaven is Far Away

BY
Julius Lester

ILLUSTRATED BY
Joe Cepeda

SCHOLASTIC PRESS · NEW YORK

Back when the world was new, heaven and earth were close together. They were so close ladders joined them and people and angels went back and forth every day like neighbors visiting one another. And if not for the snakes, it would still be that way.

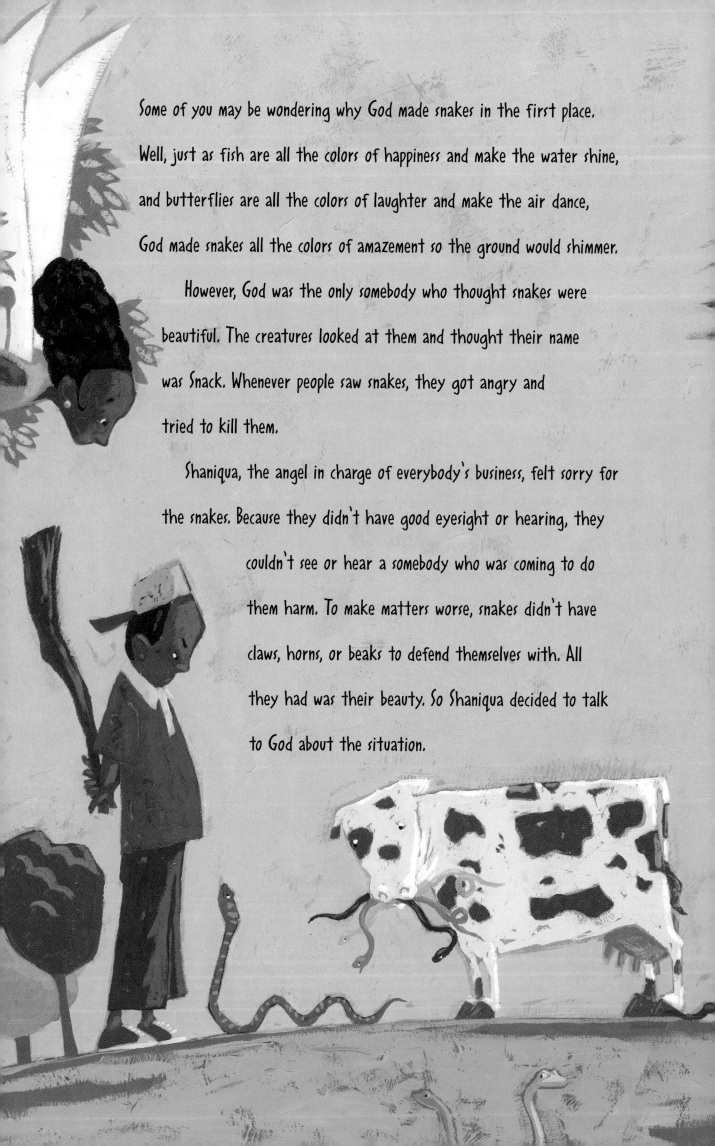

Some of you may be wondering why God made snakes in the first place.

Well, just as fish are all the colors of happiness and make the water shine,

and butterflies are all the colors of laughter and make the air dance,

God made snakes all the colors of amazement so the ground would shimmer.

However, God was the only somebody who thought snakes were

beautiful. The creatures looked at them and thought their name

was Snack. Whenever people saw snakes, they got angry and

tried to kill them.

Shaniqua, the angel in charge of everybody's business, felt sorry for

the snakes. Because they didn't have good eyesight or hearing, they

couldn't see or hear a somebody who was coming to do

them harm. To make matters worse, snakes didn't have

claws, horns, or beaks to defend themselves with. All

they had was their beauty. So Shaniqua decided to talk

to God about the situation.

God and Mrs. God (her name is Irene) were sitting on the patio finishing their second

cup of coffee when Shaniqua arrived.

"Morning, Shaniqua," God and Mrs. God greeted her.

"Morning, God. Morning, Miz God," she responded. "I came to talk about a

problem down on earth. It's the snakes."

God smiled. "I think they're the prettiest things in all the world. I love the way

they move. It's like watching silence dance."

"Yes, sir. I agree, but the creatures use snakes for between-meal snacks, and people

kill them because — well, I guess because their beauty makes people angry. And the

poor snakes don't have a way to defend themselves."

"I've got to do something

about that," God said. He took a last

quick sip of coffee, kissed Mrs. God on the cheek,

grabbed his briefcase, and set off down the golden streets

of heaven, Shaniqua running as fast as she could to keep up. As

God walked into the throne room, the Hallelujah Angelic Choir of sixtillion

voices started chanting, just as it had done every morning for the past

ninetyleven tillion years: "God! God! He's our man! If he can't do it, nobody can!"

And just as he had done every morning for the past ninetyleven tillion years, God

thought, That's true. I am the man! Smiling, he sat down on his throne and called out,

"Bruce!"

Bruce was God's secretary. He was standing in the corner brushing his wings.

"Yo! What's up, Deity?" he asked, hurrying over to God.

"Bring me some snake poison!"

Bruce had no idea what God was talking about. He flew off to the Library of Everything That Is Going to Be and typed "snake poison" on the computer.

POOF!

A big jar of a clear thick liquid appeared in his hand.

"Yuck!" Bruce exclaimed and hurried back to the throne room with the jar.

"Here you go, Mighty One!"

God gave the jar to Shaniqua. "I want you to give this

to the snakes. Tell them to put a little of it in

their mouths. The next time somebody tries

to do them harm, they can put some

poison into him or her."

"Thanks, God!"

Shaniqua

beamed.

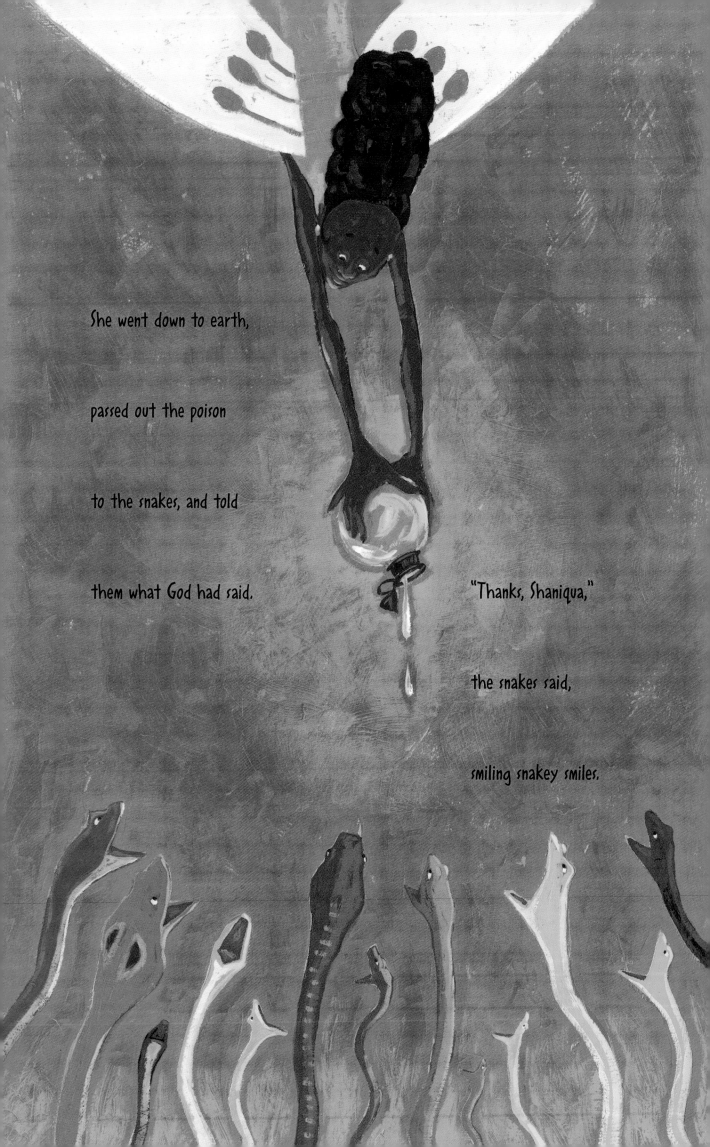

She went down to earth,

passed out the poison

to the snakes, and told

them what God had said.

"Thanks, Shaniqua,"

the snakes said,

smiling snakey smiles.

Happy that the snakes could now defend themselves, Shaniqua went home and made

herself a big glass of lemonade. But she had scarcely swallowed the first sweet sip

when Bruce came flying in, sweaty and out of breath.

"You got a problem!" he exclaimed.

"I do?" Shaniqua asked.

"It's the snakes! They're not

waiting for anyone to

do them harm."

Shaniqua's eyes narrowed.

"What are you talking about?"

"See for yourself!" Bruce answered.

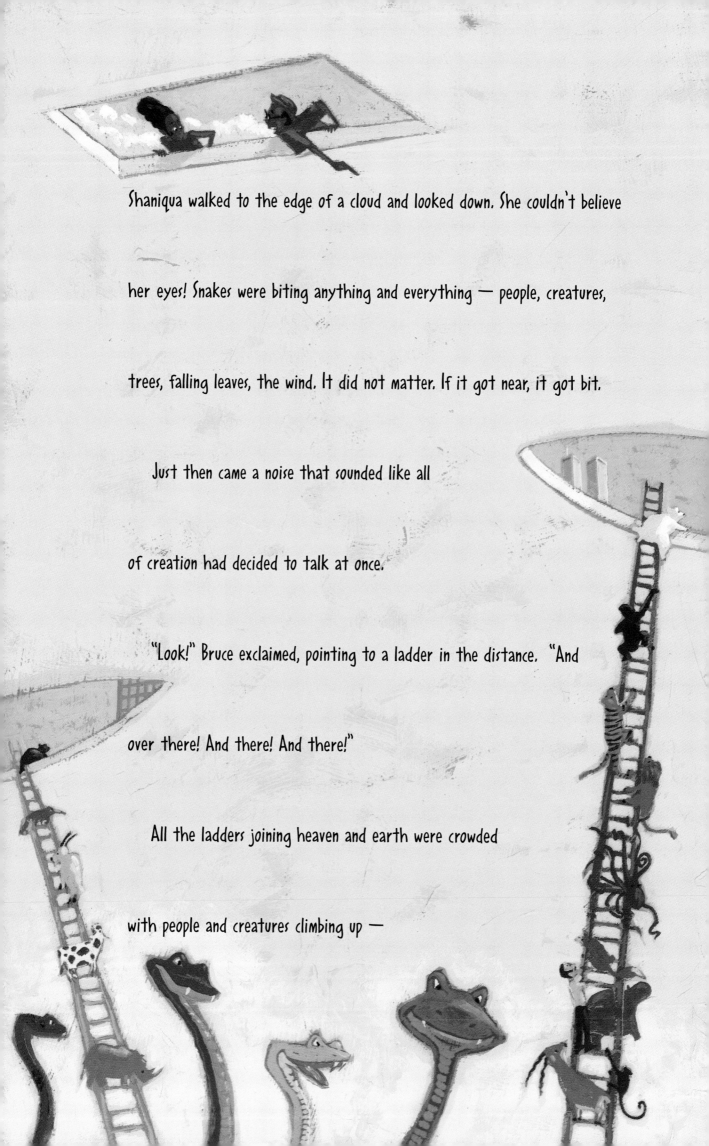

Shaniqua walked to the edge of a cloud and looked down. She couldn't believe

her eyes! Snakes were biting anything and everything — people, creatures,

trees, falling leaves, the wind. It did not matter. If it got near, it got bit.

Just then came a noise that sounded like all

of creation had decided to talk at once.

"Look!" Bruce exclaimed, pointing to a ladder in the distance. "And

over there! And there! And there!"

All the ladders joining heaven and earth were crowded

with people and creatures climbing up —

elephants,

giraffes,

hippopotamuses,

dinosaurs,

ants,

spiders,

trees,

rocks.

Over on the other side of heaven, God and Mrs. God had just started playing a game of miniature golf when he was knocked flat by a buffalo and she was run over by a herd of zebras. Three polar bears ran across God's stomach and a walrus sat on Mrs. God's nose.

"What is going on?" Mrs. God asked, sitting up and sending the walrus flying onto the back of a camel. God and Mrs. God helped each other up. They looked around. Heaven was being overrun. Everything and everybody on earth was moving to heaven!

"I don't know what's going on," God said, "but I'm going to find out.

Bruuuuuce! ShaNIIIIIQUA!"

God's voice was so loud some stars were knocked out of the sky. (By the way, those were the first falling stars, and whenever you see a falling star, well, God has just called for Bruce and Shaniqua.)

Bruce and Shaniqua hurried to God's house. "What's up, Majestic Maker?" Bruce said nervously.

"Don't you be alliterating me unless you can tell me why everything and everybody on earth is now in heaven."

"I don't know," Bruce said, then whispered, "Powerful Potentate."

God kind of liked the sound of that so he let it pass. "Shaniqua?"

"Well, I think earth is moving to heaven to get away from the snakes. They are biting anything and everything with that poison you gave them."

"I can't have everything on earth coming to live in heaven."

"Why not?" Mrs. God wanted to know.

"Bugs!" God answered.

"Good point," Mrs. God agreed. "So, what're you going to do?"

"Well, since it's the snakes causing the problem, I'll kill them and create something else to make the ground beautiful."

"You can't do that!" Mrs. God exclaimed.

"Why not?"

"Have you talked to the snakes?" she wanted to know.

"Why would I talk to the snakes? They're misusing the poison I gave them."

"Well, I'd like to know why. Let me and Shaniqua talk to them."

God sighed. "I don't see what good that'll do, but all right."

Mrs. God and Shaniqua flew down to earth and landed atop a tall mountain that a snake was biting and trying to poison at that very moment.

"Excuse us," Shaniqua said to the snake.

The snake looked up and when she saw it was Shaniqua, she smiled her snakiest snakey smile. "Oh, I am so happy to see you. Would you please thank God for us? This poison he gave us is wonderful. Now nobody steps on us or eats us."

"Yes, we know," Shaniqua said gently. "But you were supposed to use that poison only on somebody who was coming to do you harm, not on anything that shook the bush."

"But that's the problem," the snake responded. "Our eyesight is so bad that we can't tell who's coming to do us harm and who's just going to the store. And our hearing is worse than our sight. It's safer for us to put a little poison in anything that comes close."

Mrs. God smiled. "I *knew* there was a reason. Thank you for talking with us."

"Thank you for asking what it's like to be a snake. No one ever did."

Mrs. God and Shaniqua flew back to heaven and told God what they had learned.

"Well, I'll be!" God exclaimed. "You found out all that just

by talking to the snake and listening to

what she had to say?"

"We did," Mrs. God and

Shaniqua said together.

"I'll have to remember that. But we still have a problem," God said, pointing to the creatures who were continuing to climb into heaven.

"I think I know what to do but I need to confer with Shaniqua," Mrs. God said.

She and Shaniqua whispered together for a moment.

"That should work," Shaniqua said aloud.

"What'll work?" God wanted to know.

"Well, when you were creating the world you let Shaniqua create the butterflies, but I didn't get to create anything," Mrs. God said.

God looked a little sheepish. "I'm sorry, sweetheart. I didn't think you were interested."

"But you didn't ask, did you?"

God blushed. "No. No, I didn't. Bruce!"

"Yes, Feckless Fomenter."

"And what does that mean?"

Bruce shrugged. "I have no idea. I just liked the sound."

God smiled. "So do I. Write this down, Bruce: THOU SHALT
TALK TO AND LISTEN TO THY NEIGHBOR."

Bruce wrote it down. "What shall I call it?"

"The Zero Commandment. There are ten more to come."
Then he turned to his wife. "Would you like to try and
save the snakes and get earth out of heaven?"

She looked at him like he didn't have the sense he
was born with. "What do you mean, try? Do you want
me to show you how to do it?"

"Yes, dear."

And without another word, Mrs. God and Shaniqua flew to earth and Mrs. God

landed on the highest mountain on the topside of the world and Shaniqua

landed on the highest mountain on the bottomside of the world.

Mrs. God cleared her throat. Shaniqua cleared hers.

Then they opened their mouths. From Mrs. God's

throat came the rhythms of a thousand

thousand drums — bongo drums,

snare drums, conga

drums —

and from

Shaniqua's throat came

the sounds of a thousand

thousand trumpets, guitars, saxo-

phones, basses, and pianos all playing at

once, and the music and rhythms bounced off

the four corners of infinity, echoed from one end of

the universe to the other, went down to the bottom of

the ocean and out to the farthest star, spun around and

around until they spiraled inside the bodies of all the creatures and

all the people and everything that had ears and everything that didn't,

and everything and everybody started dancing. Baboons danced with racoons

and gorillas danced with caterpillars. Trees danced with geese while mountains

danced with mice. The grass was shimmying like sunshine while the waters shook

like moonshine and the rocks trembled like starshine, all dancing to the music.

Even the snakes started dancing, and as they danced, the poison left the bodies of all

but a few of them. Some of the snakes who no longer had poison got bigger as they

danced, and size became their defense. Other snakes danced until they became thin,

and speed became their defense. Other snakes danced until they became the color of

green leaves or the brown or red of earth, and camouflage became their defense.

In heaven all the creatures started dancing down the ladders because the music was

coming from earth and they wanted to be closer to it. Mrs. God and Shaniqua kept

singing until everything was back in its proper place on earth, and then they flew

back to heaven.

"Great job!" God said. "Now I'm going to give the snakes one more thing to defend themselves with."

"What's that?" Irene, Shaniqua, and Bruce asked all at once.

"Fear," God answered. "From now on people and creatures will be afraid of snakes and snakes will be afraid of them. When people and creatures see a snake, the first thing they'll try to do is run away. And when snakes come upon a person or a creature, the first thing they'll try to do is run away. But if neither one can get away, then they can go at it."

God wiggled his ears, and people and creatures went one way and snakes went the other.

Mrs. God sighed. "I'm afraid there's one more thing we have to do, God."

He looked puzzled. "What's that?"

"We've got to pull up the ladders and make sure heaven is out of reach, even

to the highest flying bird. We can't have everything on earth coming up here

whenever something goes wrong down there. They've got to work out

their own problems."

God nodded sadly. "You're right."

After the angels had pulled up all the ladders, God raised

his arms in a great sweeping motion and heaven went way, way, way up behind

the blue of the sky. (And to this day, when you see an eagle or a hawk flying at

the top of the sky, they're looking for heaven and wondering, where did it go?)

God and Mrs. God looked at each other and smiled. "It's nice having a partner to work with," God told her. They were about to give each other a kiss when Mrs. God noticed that Shaniqua was looking sad.

"Is something the matter?" she asked.

"Yes, ma'am. How can I be in charge of everybody's business if I don't know what's going on?"

God nodded. "Well, that's true. You have any ideas?"

Bruce said, "I've got an idea," and then whispered, "Marvelous Mistress."

Mrs. God smiled. "What's your idea, Altiloquent Alliterator?"

Bruce looked at Mrs. God with surprise, wondering what she had called him. But since it sounded good, he figured it was all right. "Let's build a new ladder to reach from here to there, but only we will know about it. That way Shaniqua can go to earth anytime she wants."

Mrs. God thought that was a fine idea and she gave Bruce a high-five. Then they were all slapping hands and laughing and Shaniqua invited everybody over to her place for a cookout. She had invented kosher pork chops and wanted to get God's opinion of them.

The next day,

Shaniqua and Bruce

built a long ladder

from heaven down

to earth, and

she still climbs down

often to help

people and creatures

when they

get in trouble.

My great-great-great-great

grandmother said that her great-

great-great-great grandfather's

uncle's first cousin's second wife told

her that the ladder comes down

somewhere in Africa.

Somebody else claims it's over in Asia.

But the other day, I got an E-mail that

said it had been found in South America.

But for all I know, that ladder might

touch down in your backyard

or on the roof of your building.

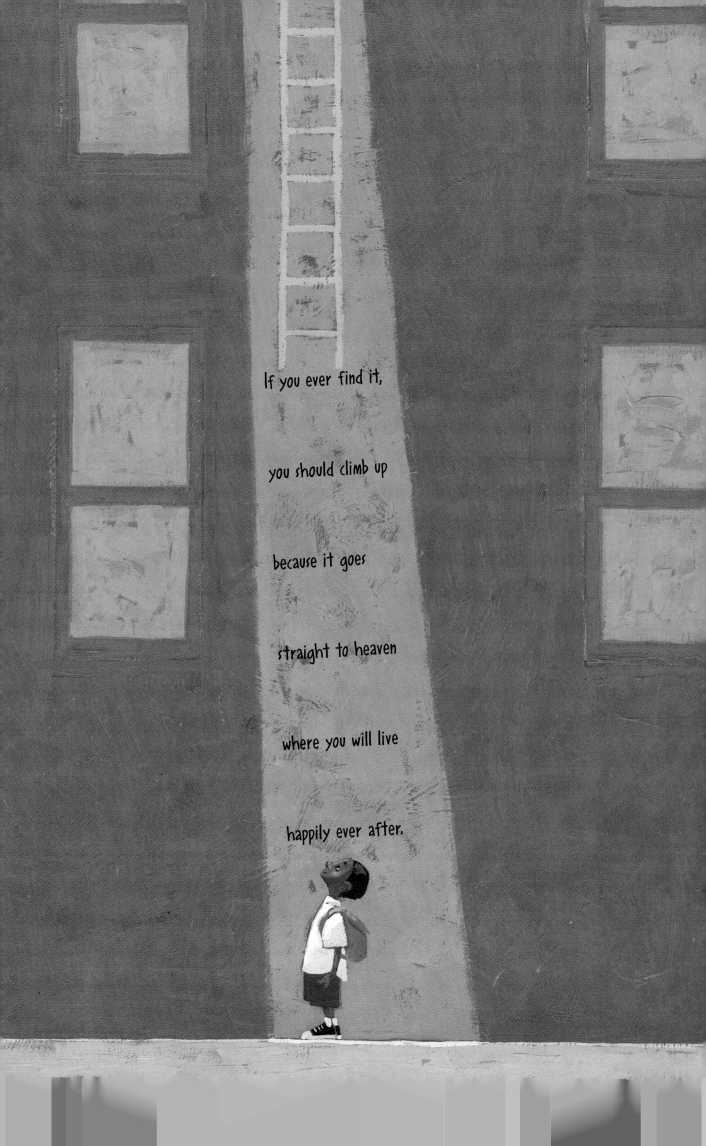

If you ever find it,

you should climb up

because it goes

straight to heaven

where you will live

happily ever after.

AUTHOR'S NOTE

This story brings together characters first introduced in *What a Truly Cool World*. In writing it, I took elements

from two folktales originally told in my book, *Black Folktales*. "How the Snake Got Its Rattles," an African-American

tale, is the story of the snakes finding themselves defenseless, climbing the ladder to heaven and being given poison

by God, and then proceeding to bite anyone who comes near. God has them return to heaven and gives them rattles

to put on their tails so they can warn anyone before they strike. I took the basic concept but expanded it to include

all kinds of snakes and an explanation of how they acquired various means to protect themselves.

The other tale is an African one, "Why the Sky Is Far Away," which I retitled "Why Men Have to Work" in *Black

Folktales*. In that story, the sky is a source of food, and people can just reach up and break off a piece of sky when

they're hungry. They become greedy and wasteful, not eating all they take, and the gods move the sky out of their

reach, which is why people have to work. From this story, I took only the idea of the proximity of earth and sky

and the moving of heaven out of the reach of earth. All other elements of the present story are original.

Julius Lester • Belchertown, Massachusetts • August 23, 2001

In memory of my father, Reverend W.D. Lester, for teaching me that God likes to laugh, too,

and Always and Evermore to my wife, Milan, whose laugh gladdens my soul. — J. L.

To all those who entered heaven on September 11. — J. C.